BLACK LIKE KYRA, WHITE LIKE ME

Story and pictures by Judith Vigna

Albert Whitman & Company, Morton Grove, Illinois

Other Books by Judith Vigna
Boot Weather
Grandma Without Me
Gregorio Y Sus Puntos
I Wish Daddy Didn't Drink So Much
Mommy and Me by Ourselves Again
My Big Sister Takes Drugs
Nobody Wants a Nuclear War
Saying Goodbye to Daddy
She's Not My Real Mother

Designed by Lucy Smith.
The typeface for this book is Avant Garde.
The illustrations were done in watercolor.

Text and illustrations © 1992 by Judith Vigna.
Published in 1992 by Albert Whitman & Company,
6340 Oakton Street, Morton Grove, Illinois 60053.
Published simultaneously in Canada by
General Publishing, Limited, Toronto.
All rights reserved. Printed in the U.S.A.
10 9 8 7 6 5 4 3 2 1

Library of Congress Cataloging-in-Publication Data

Vigna, Judith.
Black like Kyra, white like me/Judith Vigna.
p.   cm.
Summary: When a black family moves to an all-white neighborhood,
prejudice rears its ugly head as the white adults behave rudely
and children's friendships break up.
ISBN 0-8075-0778-4
(1. Prejudices—Fiction. 2. Afro-Americans—Fiction.
3. Moving, Household—Fiction. 4. Race relations—Fiction.) I. Title.
PZ7.V67B1 1992
(Fic)—dc20   92-1203
                                                           CIP
                                                           AC

For
Chris, Caroline, Helen,
Hope, David, and André,
who shared.

I used to have three best friends.
Matt and Julie were my best friends on the block.
Kyra was my best friend at the youth center.

There were a lot of drugs and shooting where Kyra lived, so her parents were trying to find a home in a safer neighborhood.

And the house next door to us was for sale.

"I wish Kyra could come and live near me so we could all play together," I told Daddy.

"Her parents might not want to leave their old friends, Christy," he said.

"They could make new ones," I told him.

"Sometimes it's hard to make new friends," Daddy said.

Next Saturday at class, Kyra told me, "A kid on my block got hurt real bad last night. Some people were shooting at each other, and he got hit in the shoulder. My mama and daddy are really scared."

"Why don't you tell them the house next door to us is for sale?" I said. "Nobody fights where I live."

"I'll tell my daddy," Kyra promised.

A few days later, Kyra's parents came to see
the house next door.

"Kyra's my best friend from gymnastics," I told
Matt and Julie. "She might come and live here."

Matt stared at his sneakers. "My dad doesn't want them on our block," he whispered.

"That's mean," I told him. "Your father never even *met* Kyra's family."

When the Kirks came out, they were all smiling. And at gymnastics, Kyra told me they were going to move in!

A few weeks later, a big truck stopped outside the house next door. I saw the Kirks and some other people unloading furniture. Kyra was all by herself on the back porch.

"Can Kyra help us with the decorations?" I asked Mommy. Our neighborhood block party was the next day, in our yard. Matt and Julie and I still had paper chains to make.

"I guess so," Mommy said.

"Are you going to invite Kyra's mother for coffee?" Mommy had invited Matt and Julie's mother when their family moved in.

"Well . . . not yet," she said. "I want to get to know her mother better first."

When Matt and Julie didn't come to my house like we planned, Kyra and I ran next door to get them.

"We can't come," Julie said. She looked at Kyra. "Our dad doesn't want us to play with you."

"Why?" I yelled. "She hasn't done anything!"

Julie gave me a funny look and went back inside. Kyra just got mad. "It's because I'm black," she told me. "My mama said some people here might not like me."

I was mad, too. What Julie said was mean.
She and Matt would be sorry they missed seeing
how Kyra made paper chains. Instead of plain
old circles, she cut out paper dolls. I painted
them. I made them black like Kyra and white like
me, and lots of other neat colors.

Mommy fixed her special lasagna for the party.

"Wait till you see the rest of the food," I told
Kyra. "Last year the neighbors brought stuff from
all the places their ancestors came from."

"I'll bet nobody cooked African," she said.

"Nobody did," I told her. "Why don't you?"

"I can make motake. That's bananas, only boiled."
Now we'd have food from everywhere!

The next evening, Daddy strung our paper chain between the lanterns in the trees. Matt's father set up a huge picnic table, and Mommy covered it with our best holiday cloth.

Soon everyone came with their dishes. There was food from lots of countries.

The Kirks came last. Kyra was holding a big bowl.

Suddenly it was very quiet in our yard.

"The Kirks brought motake, from Africa," I
explained.

"It feels like rain," Matt's father said. "Let's
go." He took Matt and Julie home. They didn't
even say goodbye.

Some other neighbors looked up and held
their hands to the sky. Then they left, too.

Kyra started crying, and her father led her indoors.

"Wait," I shouted. "The neighbors didn't mean to make you feel bad."

"I believe they did, Christy," Mrs. Kirk told me. "It was a mistake to think we could fit in here." She spoke softly, but she had a sad, hard look.

Daddy started to follow them, but then it really did rain, so we went home, too.

"How can everyone be so mean to Kyra's family?" I asked him.

"Some people are scared of anyone who looks or acts different from them, especially if that person's skin is a different color," he explained. "They don't know what to expect. They forget that what's important about a person comes from inside."

"But the neighbors can't know what Kyra and her mom and dad are like—they've never even talked to them!" I said.

When it stopped raining, we went outside to clean up.

"Oh, no!" Mommy shouted.

Something terrible had happened. The picnic table had been turned over, and all the dirty plates and bottles were scattered across our lawn. Our beautiful paper chain was stuck on the gate, with spikes right through it.

"Why *us*?" Mommy said.

Daddy said, "Seems we're being blamed for telling the Kirks about the house next door."

"You think you've got such great neighbors. Then they do a thing like *this*." Mommy looked as if she was going to cry.

I wanted to cry, too. Bad things had never happened on our block before. Why couldn't Kyra and her mom and dad live here if they wanted to?

Only the couple from across the street offered to help. Matt and Julie didn't even come to look. I'll bet their father did it.

Then Mr. Kirk arrived with a rake and some garbage bags. Daddy seemed real glad to see him.

I went next door to show Kyra our poor, ripped paper chain. "If you help me glue it back together, we can use it next year."

"We won't be coming to the next block party," Kyra said angrily. "My mama's scared. And she's mad, too. She says we don't have to take this."

It wasn't fair. What if the Kirks got so mad and scared they wanted to move away?

I ran home and told Mommy that Kyra might move. "You said you wanted to get to know her mother better, but you haven't even said hello. And Matt and Julie didn't have to be so snotty."

"They were only doing what their dad told them," Mommy said. "He's prejudiced against the Kirks because they're black. Lots of people are prejudiced sometimes, but it's not right. And what's happening in our neighborhood is scary. The Kirks must feel terrible. I'm sorry I haven't been nicer."

"I don't want Kyra to move!" I cried. "She's one of my best friends."

Mommy held me. "No rnatter what happens, you and Kyra can still be best friends," she promised.

After a while we went into the kitchen. The
Kirks were there, talking to Daddy.

"We're sorry about the neighbors," Daddy
told them. "I guess they're afraid their homes
won't be worth as much if the neighborhood is
integrated. We've worked hard so our kids could
go to good schools in a safe neighborhood."

"We have, too," Mr. Kirk said quietly.

When we went outside, another bad thing had happened! Mr. Kirk's van sat on the road like a big roosting hen. Someone had let all the air out of the tires.

Mr. Kirk wasn't quiet anymore. "What's next, firebombs?" he roared.

"This is too much," Daddy said grimly.

"I'll call the police," Mommy said. "And if you need a ride anyplace, we'll take you."

The next day, Mommy drove Kyra and me to gymnastics. It was our last class of the summer. We all made a farewell circle and danced around the gym.

I wished I could stay at the youth center forever. There, everyone was my friend.

It's winter now, and the Kirks are trying hard to
settle in.

But there's a new "For Sale" sign on our block.

Matt and Julie are moving far away.

I'm sad we'll never get to play all together.
But I still have one best friend.

And I see her more than ever.

Afro-Americans
Moving
Prejudice